Snow Dog, Go Dog

story by
Deborah Heiligman

illustrated by
Tim Bowers

SCHOLASTIC INC.

ISBN 978-0-545-68703-4

Text copyright © 2013 by Deborah Heiligman.
Illustrations copyright © 2013 by Tim Bowers. Published in the United States
by Amazon Publishing, 2013. This edition made possible under a license arrangement
originating with Amazon Publishing, www.apub.com. All rights reserved.
Published by Scholastic Inc., 557 Broadway, New York, NY 10012,
by arrangement with Amazon Children's Publishing. SCHOLASTIC and associated
logos are trademarks and/or registered trademarks of Scholastic Inc.

12 11 10 9 8 7 6 5 4 3 2 1   14 15 16 17 18 19/0

Printed in the U.S.A.   40

First Scholastic printing, January 2014

The illustrations are rendered in acrylic on gessoed illustration board.
Book design by Anahid Hamparian
Editor: Margery Cuyler

For Ketzie, and for Nancy Sandberg, who found Ketzie for us

Tinka is a play dog,
a yay dog,
a loves-to-romp-all-day dog.

A fun dog,
a run dog,
a flurries-have-begun dog.

A snow dog,
a go dog,
a running-to-and-fro dog.

A where? dog,
a there! dog,

a hiding-polar-bear dog.

A hill dog,
a thrill dog,

a wibble-wobble-spill dog.

A glide dog,
a ride dog,
a body-sledding-slide dog.

Tinka is a chilly dog,
a silly dog,

a wants-to-romp-with-Millie dog.

A play dog,
a stray dog,
a wanders-far-away dog.

A chase dog,
a race dog,

a lost-in-a-strange-place dog.

Tinka is a sad dog,
a feeling-bad dog,

a wanting-what-she-had dog.

A worry dog,
a scurry dog,
a searching-in-a-hurry dog.

A joy dog!
A boy's dog!
A here's-your-favorite-toy dog!

A clomping dog,
a stomping dog,
a having-fun-and-romping dog.

Tinka is a greet dog,
a treat dog,
a being-home-is-sweet dog.

A rosy dog,
a dozy dog,
a hugged-and-fed-and-cozy dog!